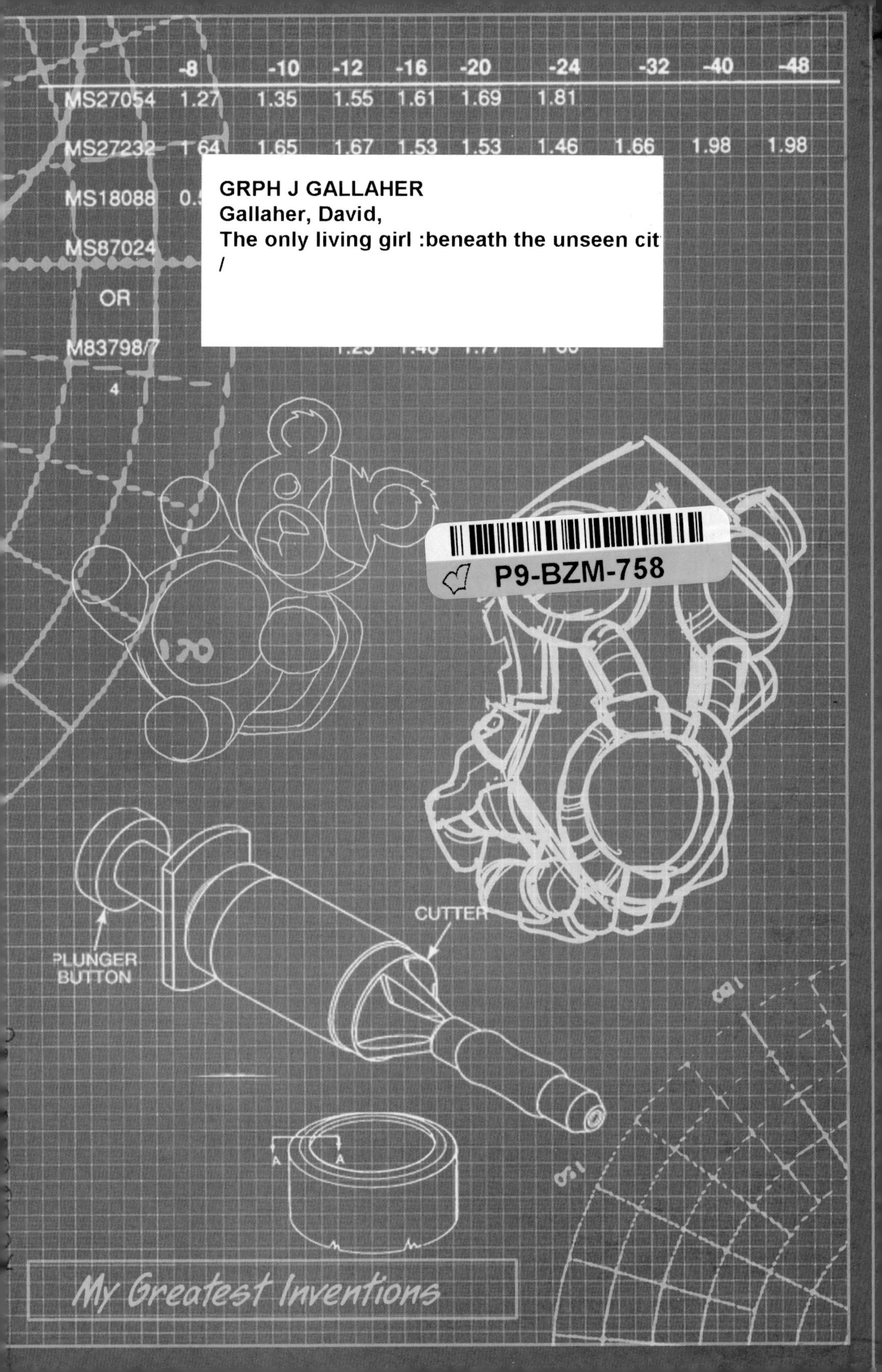
-8 -10 -12 -16 -20 -24 -32 -40 -48
MS27054 1.27 1.35 1.55 1.61 1.69 1.81
MS27232 1.64 1.65 1.67 1.53 1.53 1.46 1.66 1.98 1.98
MS18088
MS87024
OR
M83798/7
4
PLUNGER BUTTON
CUTTER
A
A
My Greatest Inventions

THE ONLY LIVING GIRL™

BENEATH THE UNSEEN CITY

by David Gallaher and Steve Ellis

PAPERCUTZ™
New York

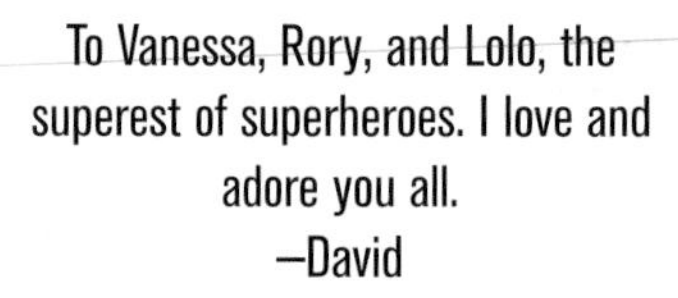

To Vanessa, Rory, and Lolo, the superest of superheroes. I love and adore you all.
–David

To my wife Yamila, beautiful and strong, who believes in me even when I can't. I love you!
–Steve

THE ONLY LIVING GIRL #2 "Beneath the Unseen City"

Chapters 3 & 4
Writer/ Co-Creator: David Gallaher
Artist/ Co-Creator: Steve Ellis
Colors: Steve Ellis
Color Flatting: Sarah Elkins, Sigi Ironmonger, Holley McKend
Color Corrections: Sarah Elkins
Lettering: Nate Pride
Studio Assistant: Jen Lightfoot
Special Thanks to Dara Hyde, Jeff Whitman, Vanessa Shealy, the tremendous team at Papercutz and all of our outstanding readers.

Serialized at: www.onlylivinggirl.com

Production – JayJay Jackson
Cover Logo – Adam Grano and Dawn Guzzo
Editorial Intern – Izzy Boyce-Blanchard
Managing Editor – Jeff Whitman
Jim Salicrup
Editor-in-Chief

PB ISBN: 978-1-6299-1055-0
HC ISBN: 978-1-6299-1056-7

Printed in China
February 2020

Distributed by Macmillan
First Printing

CHAPTER THREE

Previously in...

THE ONLY LIVING GIRL

Zee Parfitt slept through the apocalypse.

Her father, Doctor Thomas Parfitt, made a deal with a group of devilish scientists called the Consortium to save his daughter's life after a car tragically hit her. This deal saved Zee by putting her to sleep in suspended animation, but it also transformed the world into the patchwork planet of Chimerika, and warped her father into the deranged Doctor Once, who ravaged the planet's inhabitants with his evil experiments. The only living boy, Erik Farrell, and his allies vanquished Doctor Once, imprisoned Baalikar, and finally awakened Zee.

Now, six months later, Erik, Zee, her trusty companion Bear, and their Mermidonian warrior-ally Morgan are living in Stronghold and working with the newly-formed World Alliance. When a techno-organic being named Lumino arrives at Stronghold, he accidentally poisons the Alliance's Science Team with Afterall radiation. He explains that Afterall was recently discovered by the Consortium, and they are using it to destroy the world. Their planet's only hope is for Zee, Erik, Bear, and Morgan to venture across a treacherous sea to an invisible city in search of the only thing that can save them - the Primordial Intelligence.

I ALWAYS THOUGHT I WAS THE GOOD CHILD.
SO HOW ARE WE GOING TO GET UP THERE, **ZEE?**
I HAVE A PLAN.
THE ONE WITH THE PERFECT GRADES.

THE ONE WITH THE PERFECT MANNERS.
WHAT DO YOU THINK THESE INTERLOPERS WANT, BADOU?
I DON'T KNOW, AIRAVATUS.
I TRIED SO HARD TO BE THE CHILD MY FATHER WANTED.
HAVE YOU FORGOTTEN YOURSELF, YOUNGLING? THAT IS NOT AN ACCEPTABLE RESPONSE.
I WAS GOOD BUT NEVER PERFECT.
SHOULD I TRY AGAIN?
THAT ALWAYS HAUNTED ME.
YES, BUT RESPOND AS A PHILOSOPHER WOULD, USING OBSERVATION AND REASON.
AFTER ALL, IF I COULDN'T BE PERFECT...
...THEN WHAT WAS THE POINT?
WELL...

THERE IS NOTHING BEYOND PERFECT.
THEIR SHIP HAS NO WEAPONS, SO WAR DOES NOT SEEM TO BE THEIR PRIMARY PURPOSE.
PERFECTION IS A CONDITION THAT CANNOT BE SURPASSED.
AREN'T YOU OVERLOOKING THE OBVIOUS? TELL ME ABOUT THE CREATURES.
IF YOU CAN'T BE YOUR BEST AT ALL TIMES...
I BEG YOUR FORGIVENESS. I FOCUSED ONLY ON THEIR VESSEL AND NOT THE CREATURES INSIDE.
THERE WERE FOUR CREATURES. AN AQUATIC MERMIDONIAN, I BELIEVE. A WINGED CREATURE OF SOME TYPE... AND... AND...
YOU'RE ONLY GOING TO DISAPPOINT PEOPLE.
THE OTHER TWO... THEY SEEM LIKE HUMANS... BUT THAT WOULD BE IMPOSSIBLE, AIRAVATUS.
IMPOSSIBLE, ACCORDING TO WHOM, BADOU?
AND THAT'S A HEAVY BURDEN TO CARRY.

SOOOOOO.... TELL ME ABOUT THIS PLAN OF YOURS.
WELL... I HAVE A GRAPPLING HOOK IN MY GAUNTLET, **ERIK**.
WAIT... YOU HAVE A GRAPPLING GAUNTLET **AND** A TRUSTY TEDDY BEAR BACKPACK? NO FAIR.
AS MUCH AS I LOATHE TO ASK THIS...
CAN'T THAT **THING** FLY US UP THERE?
YOU CAN'T CALL IT A THING, **MORGAN**.
WELL... WHAT **SHOULD** WE CALL IT...?
WELL, DO YOU HAVE A NAME, LITTLE FELLA?

HOW ABOUT WE CALL YOU... ALZAM?
NO?
WELL... HOW ABOUT DUNGAR?
FALTON?
GORLAP?
JANAK?
MORSPON?
⊰SCOFF.⊱ THIS ISN'T WHAT WE'RE HERE FOR. WE HAVE A MISSION.
MORGAN'S RIGHT.
BESIDES, THIS CRITTER LOOKS LIKE A NEWTON TO ME, BECAUSE HIS BODY SHIFTS LIKE A NON-NEWTONIAN FLUID.
SKRITCH SKRITCH
AND SINCE NON-NEWTON ISN'T A NAME... WE'LL SHORTEN IT TO NEWTON.
HOW ABOUT IT, FELLA?
NOW THAT THIS FOOLISHNESS IS OUT OF THE WAY, CAN WE GET TO THE MATTER AT HAND?

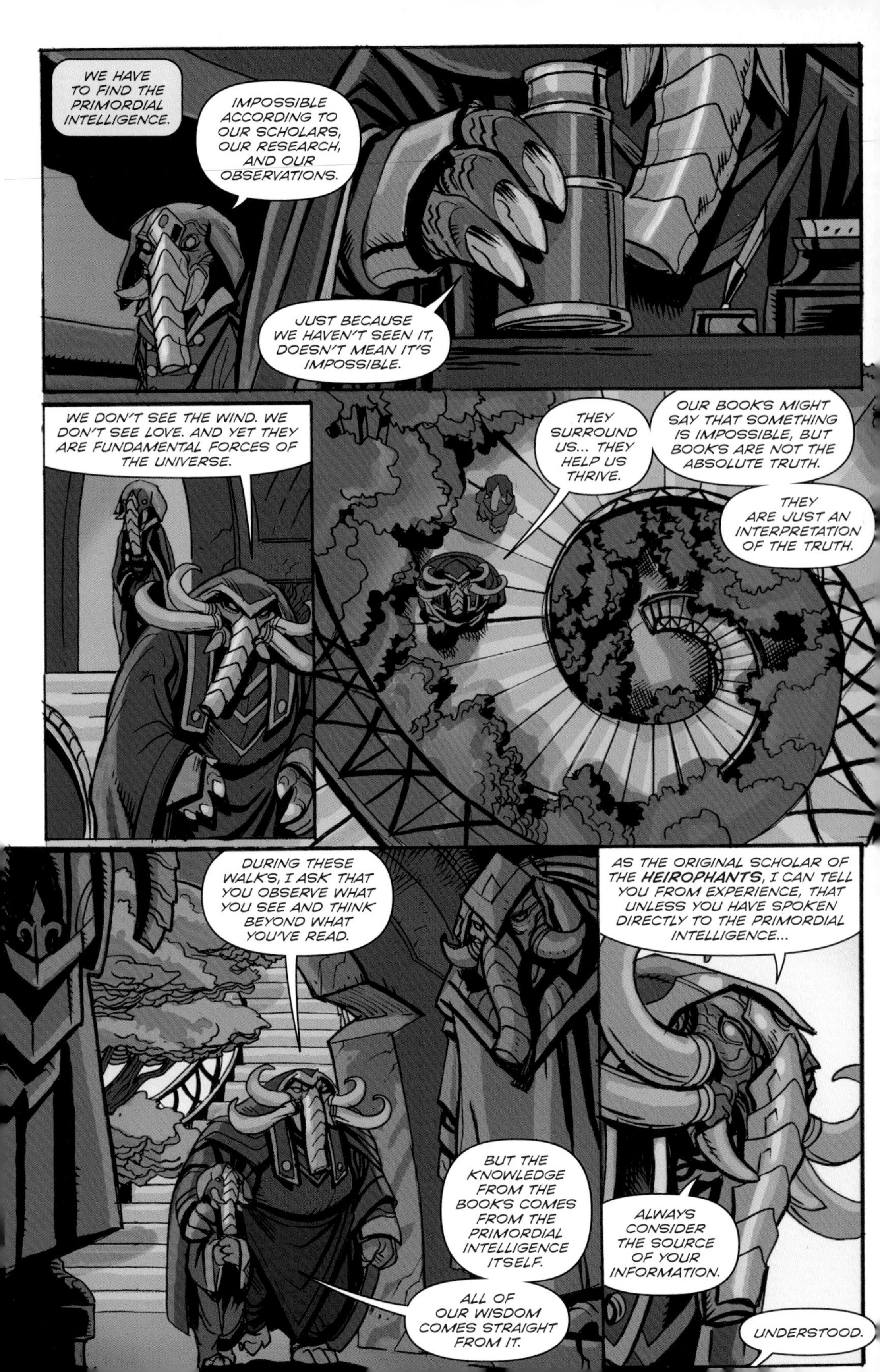
WE HAVE TO FIND THE PRIMORDIAL INTELLIGENCE.
IMPOSSIBLE ACCORDING TO OUR SCHOLARS, OUR RESEARCH, AND OUR OBSERVATIONS.
JUST BECAUSE WE HAVEN'T SEEN IT, DOESN'T MEAN IT'S IMPOSSIBLE.
WE DON'T SEE THE WIND. WE DON'T SEE LOVE. AND YET THEY ARE FUNDAMENTAL FORCES OF THE UNIVERSE.
THEY SURROUND US... THEY HELP US THRIVE.
OUR BOOKS MIGHT SAY THAT SOMETHING IS IMPOSSIBLE, BUT BOOKS ARE NOT THE ABSOLUTE TRUTH.
THEY ARE JUST AN INTERPRETATION OF THE TRUTH.
DURING THESE WALKS, I ASK THAT YOU OBSERVE WHAT YOU SEE AND THINK BEYOND WHAT YOU'VE READ.
BUT THE KNOWLEDGE FROM THE BOOKS COMES FROM THE PRIMORDIAL INTELLIGENCE ITSELF.
ALL OF OUR WISDOM COMES STRAIGHT FROM IT.
AS THE ORIGINAL SCHOLAR OF THE **HEIROPHANTS**, I CAN TELL YOU FROM EXPERIENCE, THAT UNLESS YOU HAVE SPOKEN DIRECTLY TO THE PRIMORDIAL INTELLIGENCE...
ALWAYS CONSIDER THE SOURCE OF YOUR INFORMATION.
UNDERSTOOD.

NOW, LET'S TALK ABOUT THESE INTRUDERS... AND SPECIFICALLY ABOUT THE HUMANS.
THE SCHOLARS TELL US THAT THERE WAS ONCE A HUMAN... DOCTOR THOMAS HENRY PARFITT... WHO SPECIALIZED IN QUANTUM SCIENCE.
HIS TECHNOLOGY TAPPED INTO THE AFTERALL, A FUNDAMENTAL FORCE OF THE COSMOS.
HIS STUDIES BROUGHT HIM TO THE ATTENTION OF THE CONSORTIUM, A CABAL OF MALICIOUS CREATURES.
THEY COAXED HIM INTO CREATING A GOD-LIKE BEING — BAALIKAR — A PATCHWORK EXPERIMENT MADE OF OTHER LIVING CREATURES.
BAALIKAR FORCED PARFITT TO MAKE A WORLD THAT WAS AS TAINTED AND AS VILE AS HE WAS.
PARFITT WAS TRANSFORMED BY THE CONSORTIUM INTO DOCTOR ONCE AND SACRIFICED HIS OWN PLANET TO MAKE THIS WORLD.
AS OF THE WRITINGS, NO HUMANS WERE KNOWN TO SURVIVE THE EXPLOSION.
THEIR WORLD AND HUNDREDS OF OTHERS WERE SACRIFICED.
SO BASED ON WHAT YOU'VE LEARNED, WOULD YOU SAY HUMANS... OR MORE PRECISELY, THESE INTRUDERS... POSE A DANGER TO US?
IT WOULD BE UNWISE TO JUDGE AN ENTIRE CULTURE ON THE ACTIONS OF ONE MAN... BUT, YES... I THINK THEY DO.
WELL, LUCKILY, BADOU, WE ARE PREPARED FOR SUCH DANGERS.

THE BOAT IS SECURE.
THE SOONER WE FIND THIS PRIMORDIAL INTELLIGENCE, THE SOONER WE CAN RETURN TO STRONGHOLD.
EAGER TO GET BACK TO PHAEDRUS?
NOT PARTICULARLY...
BUT WE'RE THE BEST DEFENSE OUR CITY HAS. I LOATHE THAT IT IS VULNERABLE RIGHT NOW.
MORGAN IS RIGHT.
AND JUDGING BY MY CALCULATIONS, IT LOOKS LIKE MY GRAPPLING HOOK IS OUR BEST BET TO GETTING US TO THE CITY.
SO ONCE WE'RE UP TOP, WE'LL FIGURE OUT HOW TO GET INSIDE?
PRECISELY.
VOOOSH
CLANK

ARE YOU SURE THIS IS SAFE?
SURE. I MEAN...
...I'VE NEVER TESTED IT BEFORE... BUT JUST HOLD ON TIGHTLY... YOU KNOW... JUST IN CASE.
READY, MORGAN?
IF IT'S ALL THE SAME TO YOU...
AS A WARRIOR, I MUST FOLLOW MY INSTINCTS...
KA-TING
...AND RELY ON MY OWN SKILLS.
SUIT YOURSELF...

...SEE YOU AT THE TOP.
WHAT YOU'VE TOLD ME SO FAR, BADOU, IS THAT BASED ON YOUR TEACHINGS AND YOUR OBSERVATIONS, YOU BELIEVE THESE INTRUDERS ARE DANGEROUS.
CORRECT, AIRAVATUS.
AND YOU SUGGESTED THAT NOT EVERYTHING THAT I READ IS TRUE.
WHAT I HOPE YOU GET FROM THIS LESSON IS THAT YOU SHOULD TRUST THE INFORMATION YOU RECEIVE, BUT THAT IT IS ALSO INCUMBENT UPON YOU TO VERIFY THE SOURCE OF THAT INFORMATION.
FOR EXAMPLE, TODAY WE HAVE LEARNED THAT HUMANS STILL EXIST, ALTHOUGH OUR TEACHINGS SUGGEST OTHERWISE.
WE HAVE NO KNOWLEDGE OF THESE INTRUDERS. WE DO NOT KNOW THEIR MOTIVES. WE HAVE, HOWEVER, TAKEN GREAT LENGTHS TO HIDE OURSELVES FROM THE OUTSIDE WORLD.
THESE CREATURES HAVE BREACHED OUR PRIVACY AND THEIR ACTIONS HAVE ENDANGERED US.
THAT IS TROUBLING.
WHAT SHOULD WE DO ABOUT IT, AIRAVATUS?
JOIN ME IN THE GREAT LIBRARY WHERE WE WILL CONFRONT OUR OBSERVATIONS.
IT SHOULD PROVE ENLIGHTENING.

WHEN I MAKE A MISTAKE...
THIS CRUEL VOICE HAUNTS ME.
I HOPE WHATEVER WE FIND AT THE TOP OF THIS CITY IS FRIENDLY.
IT HOVERS AROUND IN MY BRAIN, CONSTANTLY CRITICIZING EVERYTHING I DO.
BASED ON MY EXPERIENCE, ZEE...
MOST THINGS ON THIS PLANET AREN'T.
IT WHISPERS THESE PROMISES TO ME...
IF I JUST DO THINGS THE RIGHT WAY...
BUT WE HAVE MORGAN... SO WHAT COULD GO WRONG?
THE PERFECT WAY...
I GUESS YOU'RE RIGHT.
IF I STOP MAKING MISTAKES...
ZZZZZZZZZZZZZZ
EVERYTHING WILL BE OKAY.
PEEEEEEEEW
ALL OF MY FEARS AND INSECURITIES WILL DISAPPEAR.

I HOPE THAT'S TRUE.
KRRRRLUK
MORGAN!
GO GET HER, NEWTON!
I HOPE THAT I CAN BE ENOUGH...
...TO HELP OTHERS...
...WHEN THEY NEED IT MOST.

FAILURE ISN'T AN OPTION.
I'VE NEVER SEEN MORGAN TAKE A HIT LIKE THAT.
JUST KEEP AN EYE OUT FOR ANYTHING ELSE.
WHOPWHOPWHOPWHOP
WHOPWHOPWHOPWHOP
YOU MEAN LIKE GIANT MECHANICAL TENTACLES?
YES! YES! I MEAN LIKE GIANT MECHANICAL TENTACLES.
WHOPWHOPWHOPWHOP
ERIK, DON'T FREAK OUT... BUT YOU'RE GOING TO HAVE TO HANG ON TIGHT.
I'M ALREADY HANGING ON TIGHT.
TIGHTER.
WHY?
SNAP
AND... YET FAILURE FEELS INEVITABLE.

BUT I CAN'T ACCEPT ANYTHING LESS THAN THE BEST...
KRUNK
I DESERVE THE BEST.
SO DO MY FRIENDS.
OHHHHH... THAT'S WHY.
WHOPWHOPWHOPWHOP
ANY BRIGHT IDEAS?
AT THE MOMENT? NO...
ONLY COWARDS SEND MACHINES TO DO A WARRIOR'S WORK.
AND I WILL NOT BE DEFEATED BY COWARDS.

SHNNK
DO YOU HEAR ME?
I THINK EVERYBODY CAN HEAR YOU, MORGAN.
CAN YOU LET US OUT OF THESE THINGS?
JUST A MOMENT AND I'LL--
...STUPID MACHINES.
IS THAT SLEEP GAS? BECAUSE...
...because ...
...cuz ...

I AVOID TALKING ABOUT MY FEARS.
UGHH... IS EVERYONE OKAY?
I DON'T WANT OTHERS TO SEE ME AS WEAK.
WE'RE ALIVE, AREN'T WE?
I HAVE TO BE IN CONTROL OF MY FEELINGS...
LOOK AT ALL OF THE BOOKS. ARE WE IN A LIBRARY?
OR ELSE THEY WILL CONTROL ME.
MAYBE? MORE IMPORTANTLY...
WHERE IS NEWTON, BEAR, AND ALL OF OUR STUFF?
I HAVE TO PRETEND EVERYTHING IS FINE.
ALL OF YOUR QUESTIONS WILL BE ANSWERED IN DUE TIME.
BUT, LET US START WITH A QUESTION OF OUR OWN...
EVEN WHEN EVERYTHING IS VERY MUCH NOT FINE.

WOULD YOU CARE FOR SOME TEA?
WE FIND MANNERS AND SIMPLE HOSPITALITY CAN SET THE TONE FOR A PRODUCTIVE CONVERSATION.
UMMMM...
YES, PLEASE.
FINE.
MY NAME IS AIRAVATUS. THIS IS MY STUDENT, BADOU.
YOU ARE GUESTS IN OUR HOME... UNINVITED GUESTS... BUT GUESTS JUST THE SAME.
BUT EVEN GUESTS HAVE TO FOLLOW THE RULES. SO DRINK YOUR TEA AND LISTEN.

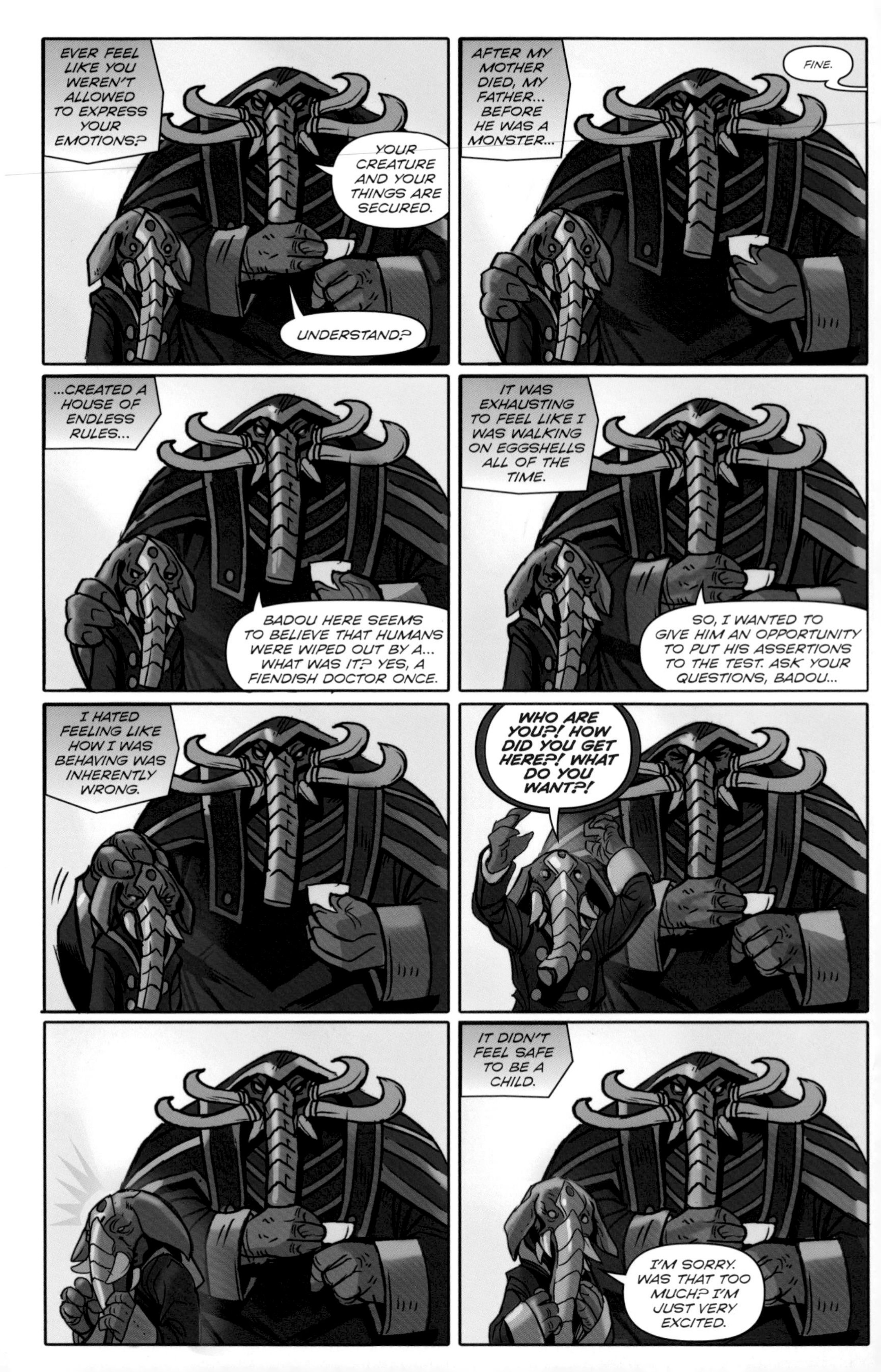
EVER FEEL LIKE YOU WEREN'T ALLOWED TO EXPRESS YOUR EMOTIONS?
YOUR CREATURE AND YOUR THINGS ARE SECURED.
UNDERSTAND?
AFTER MY MOTHER DIED, MY FATHER... BEFORE HE WAS A MONSTER...
FINE.
...CREATED A HOUSE OF ENDLESS RULES...
BADOU HERE SEEMS TO BELIEVE THAT HUMANS WERE WIPED OUT BY A... WHAT WAS IT? YES, A FIENDISH DOCTOR ONCE.
IT WAS EXHAUSTING TO FEEL LIKE I WAS WALKING ON EGGSHELLS ALL OF THE TIME.
SO, I WANTED TO GIVE HIM AN OPPORTUNITY TO PUT HIS ASSERTIONS TO THE TEST. ASK YOUR QUESTIONS, BADOU...
I HATED FEELING LIKE HOW I WAS BEHAVING WAS INHERENTLY WRONG.
WHO ARE YOU?! HOW DID YOU GET HERE?! WHAT DO YOU WANT?!
IT DIDN'T FEEL SAFE TO BE A CHILD.
I'M SORRY. WAS THAT TOO MUCH? I'M JUST VERY EXCITED.

IT DIDN'T FEEL SAFE TO BE A LITTLE GIRL.
NO -- IT'S FINE. LISTEN, MY NAME IS ZEE. THIS IS ERIK AND MORGAN. OUR LITTLE WINGED FRIEND IS NEWTON.
WE GOT HERE BY BOAT, WHICH YOU SHOT AT.
NO... I MEAN... HOW DID YOU **HUMANS** GET HERE? THE SCHOLARS SAID YOU WERE ALL... DECEASED.
YOUR SCHOLARS WERE **WRONG**.
AND... UHHH... TO PUT IT SIMPLY... WE WOKE UP HERE ON THIS CRAZY PATCHWORK PLANET.
WE'RE HERE BECAUSE OUR COMMUNITY WAS DESTROYED AND WE WERE TOLD THE PRIMORDIAL INTELLIGENCE COULD HELP.
YOU HAD NO RIGHT TO ATTACK US. WE DIDN'T DO ANYTHING WRONG.
I'LL TAKE THIS, BADOU.
WHILE YOUR CAUSE MAY BE JUST, WE HAD THE RIGHT TO PROTECT OURSELVES. I ASSURE YOU WE MEANT NO HARM, BUT...
...RATHER THAN HAVE MY WORDS SPEAK FOR ME, MAYBE IT'S BETTER YOU SEE FOR YOURSELF.
BADOU, WHILE I REPORT WITH THE **COUNCIL OF SCHOLARS**. PLEASE SHOW OUR GUESTS TO THE SANCTUARY...

...WHERE THEY CAN SEE FOR THEMSELVES HOW GRACIOUS WE CAN BE.
THIS ARCHITECTURE IS AMAZING. YOU BUILT IT ALL YOURSELF?
I DIDN'T BUILD IT BY MYSELF, ZEE... BUT MY ANCESTORS BUILT IT WITH GUIDANCE FROM THE PRIMORDIAL INTELLIGENCE.
WHAT DO YOU MEAN BY GUIDANCE?
APOLOGIES. NOT GUIDANCE, I MEAN... INSPIRATION.
WE WERE INSPIRED, THE WAY WE ARE INSPIRED BY ALL OF THIS PLANET'S CREATURES.
WELCOME TO OUR SANCTUARY.
HERE WE NURTURE, FEED AND CARE FOR RARE AND ORPHANED ANIMALS.
THAT'S SWEET AND ALL, BUT WHERE IS...
NEWTON!

THIS GROUNDING TREE WAS SELECTIVELY BRED FROM THOUSANDS OF OTHER PLANTS. NONE OF THE OTHER CREATURES ARE FOND OF ITS FRUIT.
NO OTHER MEMBERS OF ITS SPECIES HAVE BEEN DOCUMENTED BY OUR SCHOLARS.
HOW DID YOU FIND HIM?
WE DIDN'T.
SLURP
HE FOUND US.
THANK YOU FOR TAKING CARE OF HIM.
IF YOU CAN HELP US GET OUR STUFF AND POINT US TO THE PRIMORDIAL INTELLIGENCE, WE'LL BE ON OUR WAY.
I'M SORRY, BUT I CAN'T DO THAT.
WHY NOT?!

THE GREATEST TRAGEDY OF CHILDHOOD IS THAT WE'RE CONSTANTLY INVALIDATED.
I don't have permission.
WE'RE NOT...
OLD ENOUGH.
TALL ENOUGH.
PRETTY ENOUGH.
GOOD ENOUGH.
WHO DO YOU NEED PERMISSION FROM?
AFTER A WHILE, YOU START TO BELIEVE THOSE VOICES...
AIRAVATUS AND THE COUNCIL OF SCHOLARS...
AND EVERY MISTAKE YOU MAKE REINFORCES YOUR SENSE OF IMPERFECTION.
ONLY THEY HAVE THE AUTHORITY TO MEET WITH THE PRIMORDIAL INTELLIGENCE.
MAYBE YOU'RE NOT GOOD ENOUGH.
THAT'S STUPID. THEY DON'T HAVE AUTHORITY OVER ME.
LISTEN. THIS IS PRETTY URGENT.
BUT DOES IT MATTER? DO YOU JUST GIVE UP?
URGENT OR NOT. I CAN'T HELP YOU.
BUT I MAY KNOW SOMEONE WHO CAN.

IT STINKS THAT WE HAD TO LEAVE NEWTON IN THAT ZOO.
IT'S NOT A ZOO. IT IS AN ANIMAL SANCTUARY. MY HOPE IS THAT **THIS MARKET** WILL PROVIDE THE INFORMATION YOU NEED TO HELP YOUR COMMUNITY AND RELEASE YOUR WINGED FRIEND.
THAT'S ALL WELL AND GOOD, BADOU... BUT CAN YOU TELL US WHY ALMOST EVERYONE HERE IS WEARING A MASK?
MOST SOCIETIES TRADE WITH COINS, BUT INFORMATION IS A COMMODITY HERE.
NOT EVERYONE HAS ACCESS TO THE PRIMORDIAL INTELLIGENCE, SO INFORMATION AND SECRETS ARE OUR CURRENCY.
OF COURSE, NOT ALL SECRETS ARE GOOD SECRETS. SOME OF THEM BRING SHAME, HURT, AND HEARTBREAK. THE MASKS HIDE THOSE EMOTIONS FROM OTHERS.
WHEN I WAS A SMALL CALF, AIRAVATUS FOUND ME WANDERING THE STREETS OF THIS MARKET.
HE DOESN'T THINK I REMEMBER THIS PLACE, BUT I DO.
IS THIS YOUR FIRST TIME BACK?
ON NIGHTS WHEN THE COUNCIL IS ASLEEP, I SOME-TIMES SNEAK OUT AND WANDER THE STREETS.
BUT... WHY?
IT WILL BE MADE CLEAR TO YOU SHORTLY.
WE'RE HERE TO SEE **NARIA**.
NARIA: TRUTH TELLER
KNOCK KNOCK
NARIA: TRUTH TELLER
COME INSIDE, BADOU. QUICKLY.

NARIA TRUTH TELLER
SO, THE RUMORS ARE TRUE. WE DO HAVE VISITING HUMANS HERE. WHAT BRINGS YOU AND YOUR COMPANIONS HERE?
NEWS TRAVELS FAST, NARIA.
THIS IS ZEE, MORGAN, AND ERIK. THEY HAVE A MATTER THAT REQUIRES THE ATTENTION OF THE PRIMORDIAL INTELLIGENCE. I THOUGHT THAT YOU COULD HELP.
COME INSIDE. GET COMFORTABLE. HAS BADOU EXPLAINED WHO I AM OR WHAT I DO? NO?
IN THIS CITY, INFORMATION IS A COMMODITY AND TRUTH IS VALUED ABOVE ALL ELSE.
THE PRIMORDIAL INTELLIGENCE WHISPERS HIS SECRETS TO ME AND I SHARE THIS RARE GIFT WITH OTHERS.
I CAN GRANT YOU THE INFORMATION YOU NEED FOR YOUR QUEST.
MY SERVICES, HOWEVER, COME WITH A STEEP PRICE. ONE THAT FEW ARE WILLING TO PAY... AND EVEN FEWER ARE PREPARED FOR.
WHAT KIND OF PRICE?
EACH OF YOU MUST REVEAL TO ME A SECRET ABOUT YOURSELVES THAT NOBODY KNOWS.
SO... WHICH ONE OF YOU IS BRAVE ENOUGH TO START?

I'LL START.
I FIGHT BY A WARRIOR'S CODE BECAUSE WITHOUT DISCIPLINE, I FEEL MY LIFE HAS NO PURPOSE.
BUT IT HAS TAUGHT ME THAT WHEN I'M FEELING MY WEAKEST, THAT IS WHEN I NEED TO BE THE STRONGEST.
I... UM... WAS RAISED TO BELIEVE THAT BOYS ALWAYS HAD TO BE STRONG.
BUT SURROUNDED BY THEA AND MORGAN, AND NOW ZEE... I'M FEELING A LITTLE INADEQUATE.
MORGAN HAS HER SPEAR. ZEE HAS BEAR AND HER GAUNTLET. I DON'T FEEL LIKE I HAVE ANYTHING TO HELP PROTECT MY FRIENDS.
I... UMMM....
I'VE NEVER TOLD ANYBODY THIS...
BUT... I.... UMMM... KIND OF MISS...
...THE TASTE OF BIRTHDAY CAKE.
DELICIOUS FROSTING AND CANDY SPRINKLES...
...UMMM.... YEAH.

WAIT? WHAT?
MORGAN AND I REVEAL OUR DEEP DARK SECRETS... AND YOU SHARE HOW MUCH YOU MISS BIRTHDAY CAKE?
I DON'T BELIEVE YOU!
NARIA SAID THAT WE HAVE TO REVEAL SOMETHING THAT NOBODY KNOWS ABOUT US. I DID THAT.
NOBODY SAID YOU HAD TO OPEN YOURSELVES UP LIKE THAT.
WE WERE TRICKED.
THERE WERE NO TRICKS. YOU REVEALED ONLY WHAT YOU WANTED TO REVEAL, BUT BE WARY... YOUR CLEVERNESS COULD BE YOUR UNDOING.
STILL THE INFORMATION YOU PROVIDED WILL SUFFICE.
THE COUNCIL OF SCHOLARS PRIDE THEMSELVES ON BEING THE GATEKEEPERS OF ALL OF THE KNOWLEDGE THAT FLOWS FROM THE PRIMORDIAL INTELLIGENCE.
BUT THERE ARE OTHER WAYS TO ACQUIRE KNOWLEDGE.
BADOU, TAKE YOUR FRIENDS TO THE FIELD HOUSE.
THERE'S A GUARD... KOTAL... SHOW THIS NOTE TO HIM. HE'LL GRANT YOU ACCESS TO EVERYTHING.
MAY THE TRUTH GUIDE AND PROTECT YOU.

THAT'S KOTAL. HE'S ONE OF THE MOST RESPECTED GUARDS IN OUR CITY. THE FIELD HOUSE IS WHERE WE STORE OUR RECREATIONAL EQUIPMENT WHEN IT'S NOT IN USE.
OKAY, SO WE'RE JUST SUPPOSED TO GIVE THIS NOTE TO THIS KOTAL GUY AND HE'LL HELP US?
THAT'S WHAT NARIA SAID.
I WONDER WHAT IT SAYS.
DON'T OPEN IT. IT'S NOT MEANT FOR YOU.
READING IT WOULD BE AKIN TO STEALING FROM KOTAL. REMEMBER... INFORMATION IS A COMMODITY HERE.
ERIK, I THINK WE NEED TO BRING NEWTON WITH US. IS THERE A WAY THAT YOU AND BADOU CAN...
BREAK HIM OUT?
I WAS GOING TO SAY "LIBERATE HIM."
I GUESS? THINK THAT'S SOMETHING WE CAN MANAGE, BADOU?
YES. WE CAN.
GOOD. WHEN YOU DO... MEET US BACK INSIDE THE FIELD HOUSE.
MORGAN AND I WILL TRY TO GET PAST KOTAL OVER THERE.
WITHOUT GETTING CAPTURED.

BE CAREFUL, HUMAN. WE DO NOT WANT TO STARTLE THE ANIMALS WHILE THEY SLUMBER.
I DON'T GET IT, BADOU... YOU SAID YOU COULDN'T HELP US, BUT NOW YOU'RE HELPING ME RESCUE NEWTON. WHY?
I WAS RAISED ON SACRED TEXTS. IF THEY WERE WRONG ABOUT YOUR EXISTENCE... WHAT ELSE ARE THEY WRONG ABOUT?
SO YOUR CURIOSITY GOT THE BETTER OF YOU?
IN A MANNER OF SPEAKING. MY MENTOR IS VERY STRICT AND VERY GUARDED, BUT HE PRIZES LEARNING ABOVE ALL ELSE.
I THINK I CAN LEARN FROM ALL OF YOU.
WELL, I THINK WE'RE A PRETTY SMART GROUP.
COME ON, NEWTON... TIME TO GO.
YOU THINK SO TOO, RIGHT, NEWTON?
SMART... BUT DANGEROUS.
BUT WHAT'S THE PURPOSE OF KNOWLEDGE IF IT DOESN'T CHALLENGE YOU?

LET'S MEET UP WITH YOUR COLLEAGUES. BEFORE WE'RE DISCOVERED.
HELLO... KOTAL, SIR...
YES?
WE HAVE THIS NOTE FOR YOU FROM NARIA.
HUMPH.
HERE ARE THE KEYS. AFTER YOU GRAB YOUR BELONG-INGS...
THE PATH YOU'LL NEED TO TAKE IS HIDDEN BEYOND THE FAR WALL.

THIS PLACE MAKES ME UNEASY.
I KNOW WHAT YOU MEAN, IT SEEMS SOME OF THIS EQUIPMENT HASN'T BEEN USED IN YEARS.
IT GOES BEYOND THAT.
IS THIS SOME SORT OF SECRET WARRIOR SENSE YOU HAVE OR ARE YOU JUST BEING PARANOID?
WHAT YOU CALL "PARANOIA"... I CALL "INTUITION" AND IT'S WHAT'S KEPT ME ALIVE THIS LONG.
DULY NOTED.
HEY, IT'S OUR STUFF.
I'D PREFER THE TERM "ARMAMENTS."
KOTAL SAID THAT WHAT WE'RE LOOKING FOR IS BEYOND THE FAR WALL.
YOU MEAN **THIS** WALL?
HOW ARE WE GOING TO GET THROUGH IT?
DO YOU EVEN HAVE TO ASK?

WERE YOU TWO EVEN GOING TO WAIT FOR US?
OF COURSE WE WERE.
SPEAK FOR YOURSELF.
NOW THAT WE'RE ALL PRESENT AND ACCOUNTED FOR--
WHOA! LOOK AT THIS!
DO YOU EVEN KNOW HOW TO USE ONE OF THOSE?
HOW HARD COULD IT BE? PULL AND RELEASE, RIGHT?
HMMMMPH.
HOW ARE WE GETTING THROUGH?
WE'RE GOING TO SLICE IT WIDE OPEN.
READY, MORGAN?
STOP ASKING SILLY QUESTIONS.
THE HUMANS ARE BEHAVING AS EXPECTED, QUALL.

AND WITH THE ASSISTANCE OF BADOU, WE'LL GET EVERYTHING WE EVER WANTED.
AND YOU ARE STILL PREPARED TO SACRIFICE YOUR STUDENT... **YOUR GRANDSON**... TO ACHIEVE THIS GOAL?
YES. ALL OF THAT AND **MORE**...

CHAPTER FOUR

WHAT IS MORE IMPORTANT...?
TELLING THE TRUTH...?
OR KEEPING A SECRET?
I'VE NEVER MET A PRIMORDIAL INTELLIGENCE BEFORE.
NONE OF US HAVE, GENIUS.

HOW FAR WILL YOU GO TO BURY YOUR SECRET TRUTHS?
I WONDER IF IT'LL BE LIKE WHEN WE MET THEA'S MOM... QUEEN MAEYE.
YOU SHOULD HAVE SEEN IT, ZEE. IT WAS LIKE THIS GIANT HIVE MIND. ALL OF THE INFORMATION ABOUT THE CITY FLOWED THROUGH HER. IT WAS SO EASY TO ACCESS EVERYTHING.
... KNOWING THAT SOMEDAY...
HMMMM...
BADOU, THIS ISN'T THE ONLY PATH TO THE PRIMORDIAL INTELLIGENCE, IS IT?
I MEAN... CLEARLY THERE MUST BE AN EASIER WAY.
PFFFFT. EASY IS BORING.
THIS IS THE SECRET ROUTE NARIA GAVE US.
THAT'S MY POINT. WHAT IF THE SECRET ROUTE TO THE PRIMORDIAL INTELLIGENCE IS THE ONLY ROUTE TO THE PRIMORDIAL INTELLIGENCE?
...SOMEONE WILL UNCOVER THEM?

WHAT DO YOU MEAN?
YOUR CITY HAS AN ENTIRE ECONOMY BASED ON TRADING SECRETS. INFORMATION IS YOUR MOST VALUABLE RESOURCE.
IT SEEMS TO ME... IF I HAD ACCESS TO ALL OF THIS INFORMATION... I WOULD WANT TO HOARD IT AND HIDE IT FROM THE REST OF THE CITIZENS.
I MEAN... IF KNOWLEDGE IS POWER THEN WOULDN'T THE PEOPLE WITH THE MOST KNOWLEDGE HAVE THE MOST POWER?
THE COUNCIL OF SCHOLARS ARE THE ONLY ONES WISE ENOUGH TO INTERPRET THE INFORMATION FROM THE PRIMORDIAL INTELLIGENCE.
MAYBE THAT'S JUST WHAT THEY WANT EVERYONE TO BELIEVE.
KEEP IT DOWN...
MORGAN DOESN'T LIKE YOUR YAMMERING...
NOT THAT...
CHITTER CHITTER CHITTER

CHITTER
CHITTER
CHITTER
CHITTER
CHITTER
CHITTER
SHADOWRATS!
THAT!
CHITTER
CHITTER
CHITTER
WHAT THE HECK ARE SHAD-OW-RATS?
WHATEVER THEY ARE... THEY CAN'T STOP US.
WHOOSH
MY SPEAR WENT RIGHT THROUGH THE CREATURE.
TAKE COVER. I'LL EXPLAIN.
CHITTER
CHITTER
CHITTER

TRULY FASCINATING. I HAD ONLY HEARD RUMORS OF THESE CREATURES, BUT I HAVE NEVER SEEN THEM IN THE FLESH.
WHAT DID THE **RUMORS** SAY ABOUT THESE THINGS, BADOU?
LONG BEFORE WE SETTLED HERE, THIS WAS THE SHADOWRATS' DOMAIN. THEY CAME OUT NIGHTLY AND DEVOURED ANYTHING THEY COULD FIND. THEY MAY BE SMALL BUT THEIR APPETITES ARE RAVENOUS.
OKAY... BUT HOW CAN WE STOP THEM IF WE CAN'T EVEN HIT THEM?
THEY ARE INTANGIBLE, YES... BUT THAT DOESN'T MEAN THEY ARE INVINCIBLE.
THE STORY GOES THAT THEY WERE DRIVEN INTO THESE CAVERNS BY A LARGE APEX PREDATOR.
I THINK WE'RE FRESH OUT OF APEX PREDATORS.
MAYBE NOT.

I'M NOT SURE I LIKE WHERE THIS IS HEADED.
MORGAN, SEE IF YOU AND ERIK CAN CAUSE A DISTRACTION.
BADOU AND I ARE GOING TO MAKE OURSELVES AN APEX PREDATOR.
I TOLD YOU I WOULDN'T LIKE IT.
HOW BIG OF A DISTRACTION DO YOU THINK SHE WANTS?
A BIG ONE.
SHOULDN'T BE A PROBLEM.
GOOD JOB BEING USEFUL.
GLAD I CAN HELP.
CHITTER CHITTER CHITTER
CHITTER CHITTER CHITTER

AN APEX PREDATOR IS A CREATURE WITH NO NATURAL ENEMIES.
THEY EXIST AT THE TOP OF THE FOOD CHAIN.
WITH NEWTON'S MORPHING ABILITIES AND YOUR TRUNK NOISES, WE SHOULD BE ABLE TO FABRICATE OUR OWN WITH LIGHT AND SOUND.
CHITTER CHITTER CHITTER
PARDON ME, BUT WHAT DO YOU MEAN BY **TRUNK** NOISES?
YOU KNOW... LIKE AN ELEPHANT?
A WHAT?!
AN ELEP-- OH, RIGHT... YOU DON'T HAVE THEM HERE.
HERE... TRY **THIS!**
PPPPPFTTTTTTWWWWWW

NOT AS EASY AS IT LOOKS, IS IT?
NO. IT ISN'T.
HOW'S IT GOING OVER THERE, ZEE?
UMMMM... FINE. IT'S GOING FINE.
SO... UMMM... CAN YOU DO **ANYTHING** LIKE **THAT**?
I'LL TRY.
SQUEAK
THAT WON'T DO AT ALL.
HOW ABOUT YOU, NEWTON? MAYBE MAKE YOURSELF BIGGER OR SPREAD OUT YOUR WINGS?

PERFECT. NOW LET'S MAKE OURSELVES A SHADOWY APEX PREDATOR...
...WITH A LITTLE BIT OF LIGHT AND A WHOLE LOT OF LUCK.
PPPPFTTTTTWWWWW
WELL THAT WAS UNEXPECTED.
NEWTON IS JUST FULL OF SURPRISES, AREN'T YOU?
I'M NOT SURE THAT'LL KEEP THEM AT BAY FOR LONG.
YOU'RE RIGHT. WE SHOULD KEEP MOVING.

MOST OF US HOLD PAINFUL, LITTLE SECRETS...
WHOA!
I'VE NEVER SEEN ANYTHING QUITE LIKE THIS.
BUT SOME SECRETS... SOME TRUTHS... ARE JUST TOO BIG TO HIDE.
IS THAT THE PRIMORDIAL INTELLIGENCE?
I BELIEVE SO.
WAIT... THIS LOOKS FAMILIAR.
OH, MIGHTY INTELLIGENCE... I BID YOU GOOD TIDINGS. WE KINDLY ASK FOR YOUR INDULGENCE...
IT'S A MATTER OF GRAVE IMPORTANCE.

IT'S NOT ANSWERING.
THAT'S BECAUSE IT CAN'T. THIS IS JUST A FAÇADE.
THE GROUNDLINGS USE THE SAME SORT OF STONEWORK TO KEEP PEOPLE OUT OF THEIR GROTTOS.
THIS WAS DESIGNED TO SCARE US OFF.
WE DON'T SCARE OFF SO EASILY...
MORGAN, MAKE US AN ENTRANCE.
IF YOU INSIST.
WAIT...
CRACK
TOO LATE.

WHAT WE HIDE FROM OTHERS...
LET'S GO.
CAN BE JUST AS IMPORTANT AS THE REASONS WE HIDE IT.
THIS ISN'T QUITE WHAT I WAS EXPECTING.
THE TRUTH CAN BE TERRIFYING...
NO ONE EXPECTS WHAT THEY CANNOT FATHOM, ZANDRA PARFITT.
AND OVERWHELMING.
I ANTICIPATED YOUR ARRIVAL.
THERE ARE FEW THINGS IN THIS UNIVERSE THAT I DO NOT KNOW.
THEN YOU KNOW WHY WE ARE HERE.

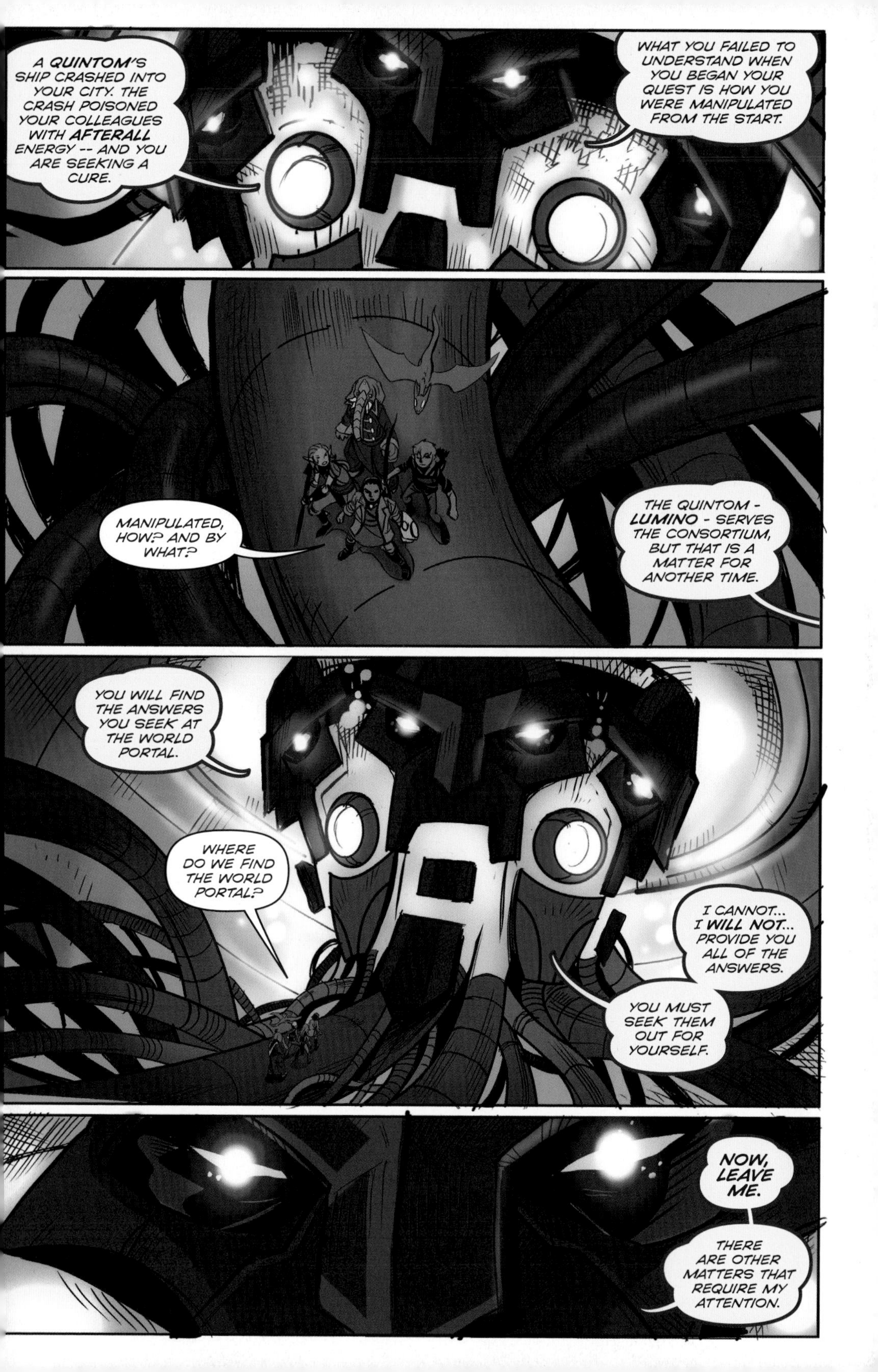
A QUINTOM'S SHIP CRASHED INTO YOUR CITY. THE CRASH POISONED YOUR COLLEAGUES WITH AFTERALL ENERGY -- AND YOU ARE SEEKING A CURE.
WHAT YOU FAILED TO UNDERSTAND WHEN YOU BEGAN YOUR QUEST IS HOW YOU WERE MANIPULATED FROM THE START.
MANIPULATED, HOW? AND BY WHAT?
THE QUINTOM - LUMINO - SERVES THE CONSORTIUM, BUT THAT IS A MATTER FOR ANOTHER TIME.
YOU WILL FIND THE ANSWERS YOU SEEK AT THE WORLD PORTAL.
WHERE DO WE FIND THE WORLD PORTAL?
I CANNOT... I WILL NOT... PROVIDE YOU ALL OF THE ANSWERS.
YOU MUST SEEK THEM OUT FOR YOURSELF.
NOW, LEAVE ME.
THERE ARE OTHER MATTERS THAT REQUIRE MY ATTENTION.

I WAS NOT PREPARED FOR THAT EXPERIENCE.
THE COUNCIL OF SCHOLARS MADE IT ALL SEEM SO DIFFERENT.
DO YOU THINK THAT MAYBE THE COUNCIL WAS TRYING TO KEEP THE TRUTH FROM YOU?
CHITTER CHITTER CHITTER
WHAT DO YOU MEAN?
I DON'T KNOW... BUT MAYBE THEY AREN'T WHAT THEY SEEM.
LET'S FOCUS ON FINDING THE WORLD PORTAL. WE CAN TALK ABOUT THE COUNCIL LATER.
THEN AGAIN... WE CAN TOTALLY TALK ABOUT IT NOW.
I BELIEVE AN EXPLANATION IS IN ORDER.

FOR DECADES, WE SOUGHT THE GUIDANCE THE PRIMORDIAL INTELLIGENCE OFFERED.
WHEN ITS INSIGHTS FAILED TO ALIGN WITH OUR GOALS, WE BURIED ALL OF THE ACCESS TO THAT KNOWLEDGE.
AND WE MADE OURSELVES THE INTELLECTUAL AUTHORITY OF THE CITY.
YOU'VE LEFT US NO CHOICE BUT TO BURY IT ALL AGAIN.
JUST LIKE WE'LL BURY YOU!
NO!
A FINE DISTRACTION.
THE LIGHT! IT'S BLINDING!

HURRY! WE NEED TO GET AS MUCH DISTANCE FROM THEM AS POSSIBLE.
ONCE NEWS TRAVELS... AND IT TRAVELS FAST... THERE WILL BE VERY FEW PLACES WE CAN HIDE.
I HATE HIDING.
BUT THE REST OF YOU ARE SO FRAGILE.
TWAK
FRAGILE OR NOT, WE SHOULDN'T HAVE TO HIDE. WE UNCOVERED THE TRUTH ABOUT THIS CITY!
BUT IT WAS A TRUTH PEOPLE WEREN'T READY TO HEAR.
WAIT... THAT GIVES ME AN IDEA.
THINK WE CAN LOSE THESE FOLKS IN THE MARKET?
WHY WOULD WE GO TO THE--
...OH... I DO LIKE THE WAY YOU THINK, ZEE...

I LIKE IT VERY MUCH INDEED.
HOW FAR IS NARIA'S FROM HERE?
NOT MUCH FARTHER.
WHY ARE WE HEADED BACK THERE?
WELL, IF ANYBODY WOULD KNOW ABOUT SOME SORT OF SECRET PORTAL...
IT'D BE HER.
THESE GUARDS TRY MY PATIENCE.
QUICKLY. THIS WAY.
KNOCK KNOCK KNOCK
COME INSIDE, BADOU. QUICKLY.

SO UNEXPECTED TO SEE YOU AND YOUR COMPANIONS AGAIN, BADOU.
TO WHAT DO I OWE THE PLEASURE?
MY FRIENDS AND I FOUND THE PRIMORDIAL INTELLIGENCE. THE TRUE PRIMORDIAL INTELLIGENCE. THE COUNCIL OF SCHOLARS HAS BEEN LYING TO US FOR YEARS.
OH, BOTHER. I HAD SUSPECTED AS MUCH.
AND YOU ARE HERE BECAUSE YOU NEED MY HELP?
THE INTELLIGENCE SAID WE HAD TO FIND THE WORLD PORTAL... BEFORE WE HAD A CHANCE TO EVEN FIGURE OUT WHAT THAT IS... AIRAVATUS SENT HIS GUARDS AFTER US.
GUARDS THAT COULD VERY WELL BE ON THEIR WAY HERE NOW.
PFFT. I COULD TAKE THEM.
YOUR NEWS IS QUITE DISTRESSING, BUT I CAN HELP YOU FIND THE WORLD PORTAL.
THE QUESTION IS... WHO IS PREPARED TO PAY THE PRICE?

I AM.
A SECRET FOR A SECRET, RIGHT?
THAT IS CORRECT.
I WILL SHARE MY SECRET WITH YOU, IF YOU TELL MY FRIENDS WHERE THEY CAN FIND THE WORLD PORTAL.
HOW VERY SELFLESS OF YOU. PROCEED.
I... BADOU BAHJAT... I KNOW...
KNOW THAT YOU... NARIA DEJEAN... ARE MY MOTHER.

I KNOW THAT AS A CALF, MY GRANDFATHER AIRAVATUS KIDNAPPED ME FROM THE MARKET AND RAISED ME AS HIS OWN.
I DON'T KNOW WHY HE DID WHAT HE DID, BUT I HAVE SPENT MANY EVENINGS IN THIS MARKET... TRADING SECRETS... TRYING TO FIND WHAT BECAME OF YOU.
I HAVE KNOWN FOR SOME TIME... BUT WAS NEVER BRAVE ENOUGH TO SAY ANYTHING UNTIL NOW.
OH, BADOU.
I WISH THINGS WEREN'T SO COMPLICATED.
BUT, I'M SO GLAD YOU KNOW THE TRUTH.
I HAVE MISSED YOU SO MUCH.
BANG
BANG
BANG
WE KNOW YOU'RE IN THERE!
SURRENDER NOW!

QUICKLY... HOW DO WE GET TO THE WORLD PORTAL?
SURRENDER NOW!
YOU'LL FIND WHAT YOU ARE LOOKING FOR IN AIRAVATUS' STUDY.
YEAH, BUT HOW ARE WE GOING TO GET PAST THE GUARDS?
YOU'RE NOT GOING TO GO PAST THEM...
YOU'RE GOING TO GO UNDER THEM.
A TRAP-DOOR? SWEET.
FOLLOW THIS PASSAGE ALL THE WAY DOWN AND YOU'LL GET TO WHERE YOU NEED TO BE.
BADOU AND I WILL BUY YOU SOME TIME.
GO QUICKLY.
BANG BANG

IS THIS THE PLACE?
YES, THIS IS WHERE NARIA SAID WE'D FIND THE WORLD PORTAL.
HOW DO WE EVEN KNOW WHAT IT IS SUPPOSED TO LOOK LIKE?
I'M SURE WE'LL KNOW WHEN WE FIND IT.
I BETCHA IT'LL LOOK ALL SCIENCE-Y AND STUFF.
IT'S NOT HERE.
NOT HERE EITHER, BUT KEEP LOOKING.
CLICK
OKAY, THAT WAS A FREEBIE.

THIS ISN'T WHAT I WAS EXPECTING.
ME EITHER. AND YET... THE TECHNOLOGY SORTA REMINDS ME OF DOCTOR ONCE'S LAB.
CAN WE PLEASE NOT USE THAT NAME?
SORRY, ZEE... I JUST MEANT... THIS LOOKS LIKE THE SORTA TECH YOUR FATHER DEVELOPED.
I'D LIKE TO REMIND YOU THAT WE HAVE ANGERED THIS ENTIRE CITY.
AND WHILE I COULD TAKE THEM ALL ON, WE HAVE A MISSION TO COMPLETE.
MORGAN IS RIGHT. WE HAVE TO GET BACK TO STRONGHOLD BEFORE THE GUARDS GET TO US.
UMMMM... I COULD BE WRONG... BUT I THINK I FOUND IT.
ARE YOU SURE THIS IS THE WORLD PORTAL?
ONLY ONE WAY TO FIND OUT.
TECHNICALLY, I'M SURE THERE IS MORE THAN ONE WAY TO FIND OUT.
WE DON'T HAVE TIME FOR "TECHNICALLY."
COME ON.
UMMM... IS THERE A BUTTON OR SOMETHING WE'RE SUPPOSED TO PUSH?

I GUESS NOT.
WHERE ARE WE?
I DON'T KNOW, BUT I'M DETECTING A HUGE AFTERALL ENERGY SIGNATURE.
COULD YOU FIND OUT FAST?
I THINK WE HAVE COMPANY.
STATEMENT: I AM THE EYE OF INTERROGATION.
QUERY: I AM THE EYE OF INTERROGATION.
WE DON'T HAVE TIME FOR THIS.
TSSST

I'M NOT SURE THAT WAS NECESSARY.
LET'S AGREE TO DISAGREE.
I THINK ZEE IS RIGHT, MORGAN. WE STILL HAVE NO IDEA WHERE WE ARE....
SO LET'S TRY NOT TO BREAK THINGS JUST YET.
FINE.
SPEAKING OF WHICH, I'M GETTING THE IDEA THAT WE'RE IN A LAB OR TESTING FACILITY OF SOME SORT.
NOW THAT YOU MENTION IT, IT DOES FEEL WEIRDLY... I DUNNO... STERILE?
THEA AND I WERE--
SURRENDER OR BE DESTROYED.

FAILURE TO COMPLY WILL RESULT IN TERMINATION.
I'M NOT SURE I LIKE THOSE OPTIONS.
INTRUDERS ARE NOT IN COMPLIANCE. ANNIHILATION PROTOCOLS ACTIVATED.
ZPPPPT
CAW!
CAN ONE OF YOU DRAW IT'S FIRE?
CRUUUUK
ZPPPPT
ZPPPPT
ZPPPPT

THAT'S MORE LIKE IT.
I'M GOING TO TRY AND JAM ITS SIGNAL.
NEWTON, TAKE EVASIVE ACTION.
NO... YOU'VE LEFT ZEE WIDE OPEN.
UUUUUUUUUUUUURRRRRRNNN
ZEE!

BWWWTZ
AHHHHHHH!
MORGAN!
ALMOST... GOT IT....
ZRRT
CLANK
SHE'S IN PRETTY BAD SHAPE.
LET'S SEE IF WE CAN GET HER OUT OF HERE.

CRUNCH
COME ON, MORGAN...
SNAP
GRUNT!
BZZZZZZZZT
Nooooooooo...

LIKE I SAID, THE TRUTH CAN BE SCARY...
IT'S IMPOSSIBLE... I SAW DOCTOR ONCE DIE.

NOTHING IS IMPOSSIBLE WITH SCIENCE.
FATHER?

...BUT IT ALWAYS COMES OUT IN THE END.
NOT EVEN CLOSE.
MY NAME IS DOCTOR TWICE.

WATCH OUT FOR PAPERCUTZ

Welcome to the second, spine-tingling THE ONLY LIVING GIRL graphic novel, “Beneath the Unseen City,” by writer/co-creator David Gallaher and artist/co-creator Steve Ellis, brought to you by Papercutz, the Earth-bound tribe of humans dedicated to publishing great graphic novels for all ages. I'm Jim Salicrup, the Editor-in-Chief and Patchwork-Person, here to help newcomers to this strange wonderful world of THE ONLY LIVING GIRL…

It all began with the critically-acclaimed THE ONLY LIVING BOY webcomic by David Gallaher and Steve Ellis. It was in this webcomic that everything regarding Erik Farrell and Zee Parfitt started. If you've been following the Papercutz graphic novels, then you're already up-to-speed, but for those of you just joining us, it's easy to catch up. You can go to www.the-only-living-boy.com and that'll take you through the story of Erik Farrell, THE ONLY LIVING BOY.

Or you could pick up the five volume THE ONLY LIVING BOY series available at booksellers everywhere and at your local public or school library. These books collect the webcomic in five volumes.

Or you could get THE ONLY LIVING BOY OMNIBUS, which not only collects the five graphic novels, but includes THE ONLY LIVING BOY FREE COMIC BOOK DAY comic and features another all-new THE ONLY LIVING BOY story. This book is also available at booksellers everywhere and at your local public or school library.

Following THE ONLY LIVING BOY series is THE ONLY LIVING GIRL, focused on Zee Parfitt. Once you've caught up on THE ONLY LIVING BOY, then all you need is the first THE ONLY LIVING GIRL graphic novel, and you're totally up to speed. Even if you missed that, don't worry, as there's a handy re-cap on page 4 that gives you everything you'll need to know to enjoy “Beneath the Unseen City.”

Most Papercutz graphic novels are self-contained, meaning they tell a complete story or several stories all in one graphic novel. But THE ONLY LIVING GIRL is a little different. Like the blockbuster Marvel movies, where each movie (except for that Avengers 2-parter) tells a complete story, each of THE ONLY LIVING GIRL graphic novels tells a complete story, but it's also a piece of a much bigger story. The good news is, that unlike Marvel, you don't need to catch up on eighty years of comics or ten years of movies – this is just the six graphic novels chronicling the adventures of Erik and Zee! Shouldn't take that long to catch up, right?

In fact, knowing how bright our fans are, we imagine that six graphic novels isn't quite enough to completely satisfy your appetite for extraordinary adventure stories. Well, ever-thinking Papercutz was able to anticipate that this might be a concern, and we're happy to announce two new Papercutz series that will rocket you to the future and plummet you back to the past for more action, adventure, and fun! First, there's…

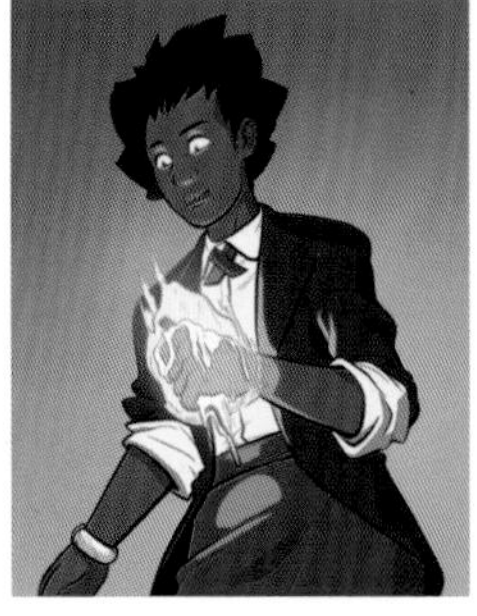

SCHOOL FOR EXTRATERRESTRIAL GIRLS – An all-new graphic novel series co-created by Jeremy Whitley, writer (he's the creator of *Princeless*, and the writer of Marvel's *Future Foundation*) and Jamie Noguchi, artist, about a 15-year-old girl, Tara Smith, who suddenly discovers that everything she thought she knew about herself was a lie. That she's not even a human being – that she's actually an alien. And that's when she finds herself enrolled in the SCHOOL FOR EXTRATERRESTRIAL GIRLS.

Then there's…

ASTERIX – If this series sounds familiar, it may be because ASTERIX is one of the most popular and best-selling comics series in the world. Created by René Goscinny, writer, and Albert Uderzo, artist, sixty years ago, Papercutz is proud to become the new North American publisher of this classic comics series. Asterix, for those of you who may be unfamiliar with him, is a scrappy warrior in a small village in Gaul, in the year 50 BC. Somehow Asterix and his village have managed to fend off the Roman Empire from conquering them. How could this tiny warrior and this tiny village possibly survive against such overwhelming odds? Turns out they have a secret weapon – a power potion that gives every member of their village super-strength. That doesn't stop the Romans from trying to defeat Asterix and his friends… and the stories of their endless battles are both exciting and lots of fun. Asterix also has plenty of other adventures back then as he travels all over the world and you can experience them all in ASTERIX, as well.

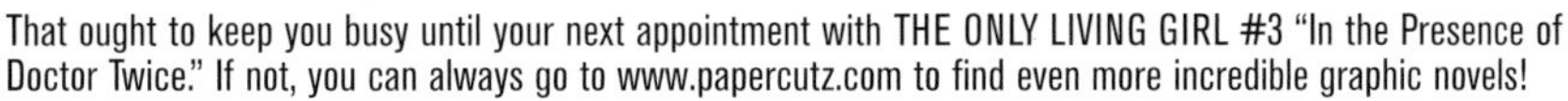

That ought to keep you busy until your next appointment with THE ONLY LIVING GIRL #3 “In the Presence of Doctor Twice.” If not, you can always go to www.papercutz.com to find even more incredible graphic novels!

Thanks, Jim

STAY IN TOUCH!

EMAIL: salicrup@papercutz.com
WEB: papercutz.com
INSTAGRAM: @papercutzgn
TWITTER: @papercutzgn
FACEBOOK: PAPERCUTZGRAPHICNOVELS
FAN MAIL: Papercutz, 160 Broadway, Suite 700, East Wing, New York, NY 10038

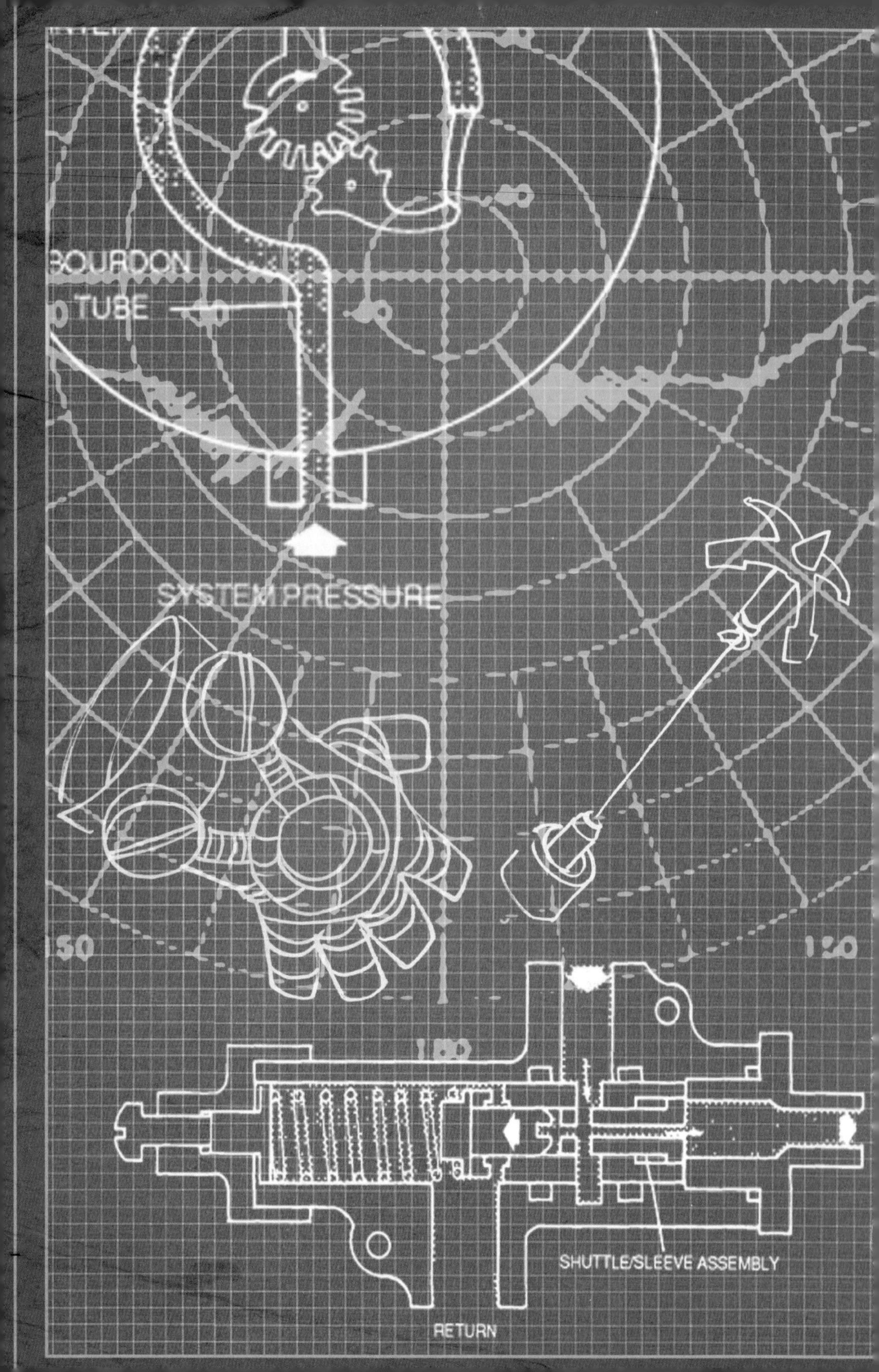
BOURDON
TUBE
SYSTEM PRESSURE
150
120
SHUTTLE/SLEEVE ASSEMBLY
RETURN